Lila and Myla
the Twins
Fairies

To Greta and Emile

Special thanks to
Rachel Elliot

ORCHARD BOOKS
338 Euston Road, London NW1 3BH
Orchard Books Australia
Level 17/207 Kent Street, Sydney, NSW 2000
A Paperback Original

First published in 2014 by Orchard Books

HiT entertainment

A CIP catalogue record for this book is available
from the British Library.

ISBN 978 1 40833 066 1

3 5 7 9 10 8 6 4

Printed and bound by CPI Group (UK) Ltd, Croydon, CR0 4YY

The paper and board used in this paperback are natural recyclable
products made from wood grown in sustainable forests. The
manufacturing processes conform to the environmental regulations
of the country of origin.

Orchard Books is a division of Hachette Children's Books,
an Hachette UK company

www.hachette.co.uk

Lila and Myla
the Twins
Fairies

by Daisy Meadows

ORCHARD

www.rainbowmagic.co.uk

The Fairyland Palace

Lila & Myla's Cottage

Tippington Town

Jack Frost's Spell

I will not sleep nor rest my head
Till fairy hearts are filled with dread.
Soon twins around the world will find
They've left their happy days behind.

This spell makes me a work of art;
Twice as mean and twice as smart.
The king and queen will both be lost
And Fairyland will turn to frost!

Lila's
Pendant

Contents

Party Pairs

"This is the house," said Rachel Walker, pointing up at a tall, white townhouse.

A bunch of pink balloons was tied to the gate, and there was another bunch pinned to the front door. Rachel smoothed down her party dress and smiled at her best friend, Kirsty Tate. Kirsty was staying with Rachel for the half-term holidays.

"It was really kind of your friends to invite me to their birthday parties," said Kirsty. "I've never been to two in one day before!"

Rachel's school friends Jessy and Amy were twins, and they were having two separate birthday parties – one for each of them.

"Jessy and Amy's parents are really good fun," Rachel said as they walked up to the front door. "They're letting Jessy have her party this morning, and Amy have hers this afternoon. The twins like different music and decorations, and their mum and dad wanted to make sure they were both happy!"

She knocked on the door and it was opened by a pretty girl with long blonde hair and big blue eyes. She was wearing a sparkly pink party dress and there was a pink bow in her hair.

"Happy birthday, Jessy!" said Rachel.

"Thanks," said Jessy with a smile. "This must be Kirsty? Hi!"

"Hi, and happy birthday," said Kirsty.

Jessy invited them in. There were pink
balloons pinned into every corner and
the guests were dancing to pop music.
A table was piled high with presents
wrapped in pink paper.

"Those are the prizes for the party
games," Jessy said, seeing Rachel looking
at them.

Kirsty peeped into the kitchen and saw a tray full of pink jellies on the dining table.

"Pink's my favourite colour," said Jessy with a smile. "Can you tell?"

The girls laughed and gave Jessy their presents. Then another girl came over and gave Rachel a hug.

"Happy birthday, Amy," said Rachel with a smile. "Kirsty, this is Amy – Jessy's twin."

"Goodness, you don't look alike!" said Kirsty in surprise.

Amy's blonde hair was cut into a
bob, and she was wearing
cropped jeans and a
red T-shirt. She
laughed and
linked arms with
her sister.

"We're
identical twins,
but we're very
different," she
said. "Luckily
our parents let us
be ourselves! Come on, let's start playing
some games."

The first game was Musical Chairs. It
was a lot of fun, but suddenly the CD
started to skip. While Jessy's dad tried to
fix it, her mum went to the prizes table.

"We might as well end the game now and start on the jellies," she said. "Oh no! Where have all the prizes gone?"

The table was completely empty. Jessy's father frowned.

"Someone must have moved them," he said. "I'll go and look in the kitchen."

But when he went into the kitchen, he let out a shout of surprise.
Rachel and Kirsty hurried after him, followed by the rest of the party guests.

They saw a terrible mess. The bowls
of beautiful pink jelly had been tipped
upside down and trampled into the
kitchen mats. Paints and glitter from the
crafts table in the corner had also been
emptied all over the floor.

While everyone was exclaiming and wondering what had happened, Kirsty tugged on Rachel's arm.

"Look over there," she whispered.

There was a large footprint in some spilled purple glitter, and the girls recognised it at once.

"It's a goblin print!" whispered Rachel.

Jessy's dad folded his arms. He suddenly looked very grumpy.

"If Jessy's party is going to be this much trouble, we might have to cancel Amy's party," he said.

"I agree," said Jessy's mum, frowning. "Suddenly I'm feeling very tired."

Jessy and Amy looked very upset.

"Our birthday is turning into a disaster!" cried Amy.

19

Seeing Double

Jessy's parents walked back into the sitting room and the guests followed. Rachel held back, looking puzzled.

"I've never heard Jessy's mum and dad sound so cross," she said.

Just then, a green balloon floated past them towards the open back door. It bobbed out into the garden.

"That's odd," said Kirsty. "I thought that all Jessy's balloons were pink."

"They were," said Rachel. "Oh Kirsty, do you think that there are goblins here? After all, green's their favourite colour!"

Rachel and Kirsty knew all about goblins, because they were friends with the fairies. Jack Frost liked sending his goblins to cause trouble for the fairies, and Rachel and Kirsty had often helped their magical friends defeat him.

"Let's follow the balloon," said Kirsty. "If it is goblins, there's bound to be more trouble."

The girls ran out into the garden and spotted the balloon bobbing away behind a wooden shed. They ran around the corner of the shed and found a little garden pond. Two garden gnomes were standing beside it with toy fishing rods.

"Look, there's the balloon," said Rachel. "There's definitely something magical about it."

It was hovering beside the shed wall, even though there was a little breeze

that should have blown it away. As the girls watched, it began to grow bigger and bigger. Then... POP! The balloon disappeared and two tiny fairies were fluttering towards Rachel and Kirsty.

"Hello, I'm Myla," said the little fairy on the left.

"And I'm Lila," said the fairy on the right.

Rachel and Kirsty blinked, hardly able to believe their eyes. The fairies were both wearing pale orange shorts, pink jackets and  sparkly ankle boots. They both had short black hair, but Myla had pink highlights and Lila had blue.

"We're the Twins Fairies!" they said together.

"Oh, it's wonderful to meet you both," said Kirsty.

"I'm so glad it was you in the balloon," said Rachel. "We thought that it might be something to do with the goblins."

She explained about the problems at the birthday party and the goblin footprint.

"That's why we're here," said Lila in a serious voice. "The queen sent us from Fairyland to ask for your help."

"We're always happy to help Fairyland in any way we can," said Rachel.

"What's happened?"

"It's Jack Frost," said Myla, sounding gentler than her twin. "He and his goblins crept into our cottage yesterday while we were out. They stole some very precious magical objects from us."

"And without them, things are going to go terribly wrong for twins everywhere," finished Lila. "You see, we look after twins all over the human world and in Fairyland."

"Is that why things started to go badly at the party?" asked Kirsty. "Presents disappeared and the music stopped."

The twins nodded.

"It's all Jack Frost's doing," said Myla with a sigh.

"What are your magical objects?" Rachel asked.

"First there's the heart pendant," said Lila. "I own one half and Myla owns the other. My half makes sure that people treat twins as individuals, and Myla's half makes sure that twins have fun being twins."

"Jack Frost also took our Gemini ring," said Myla. "It ensures that twins aren't compared with each other all the time."

"Will you help us to find our magical objects?" asked Lila.

"Of course," said Kirsty at once. "But how shall we—"

She broke off because she heard a strange, high-pitched giggle coming from the pond.

"Look!" cried Rachel, pointing to where they had seen the garden gnomes fishing. "One of the gnomes has disappeared!"

"No, he hasn't..." said Lila.

She swooped down to some tall grasses beside the pond and pushed them aside. A goblin was crouching down behind them.

"That wasn't a gnome at all," Kirsty exclaimed.

"It was a goblin in disguise!"

The goblin leapt over the tall grass and raced away from them.

"Follow that goblin!" cried Lila.

Tricked!

The girls raced after the goblin, who darted into the garden shed and slammed the door shut. Rachel pushed on the door, but it wouldn't open.

"I think he's leaning against the door," she said.

"We need to ask him what he knows about our magical objects," said Myla.

31

"If we both push together, we might be stronger than him," said Kirsty. "Let's try."

Rachel and Kirsty pushed on the shed door with all their strength. Myla and Lila pushed too, fluttering as hard as they could against the top of the door.

They heard a squawk from inside, then the door gave way and they all tumbled inside.

"There he is!" cried Lila.

The goblin was trying to hide under an old stripy parasol.

"We can see you," said Kirsty. "Please come out of there — we want to ask you some questions."

The goblin threw the parasol to one side and sat down on an upturned flowerpot. He folded his arms and looked very grumpy.

"I'm not talking to humans or fairies," he said. "You're all the same. Tricksy!"

"We just want to know why Jack Frost took the Twins Fairies' magical objects," she said.

"And where he's hidden them," added Kirsty hopefully.

"Shan't tell you," said the goblin.

He stuck out his tongue and stood up.

"Let me past," he said. "I want to go and eat more of those jellies."

"There are no jellies left," said Rachel. "Besides, we're not moving until you have answered our questions."

The goblin sat down again and stroked his chin thoughtfully.

"Let me think…" he muttered.

The girls waited. Myla and Lila were fluttering above them, staring hopefully at the goblin. He opened his mouth, and then they all heard the church clock strike. The goblin put his head on one side as if he were counting. The clock chimed twelve times, and then the goblin gave a little giggle.

"Twelve o'clock," he said, rubbing his bony hands together in glee. "That's my job done."

"What do you mean?" Lila demanded.

"Jack Frost has had enough of you all interfering in his plans," said the goblin. "I just had to make sure that you didn't take the humans to Fairyland until after twelve o'clock. That way, Jack Frost knew you would be too late to stop him!"

The Twins Fairies groaned, but Kirsty had an idea.

"You were very clever to trick us like that," she said to the goblin. "You had us completely fooled."

"I'm the best actor of all the goblins in the Ice Castle," said the goblin in a boastful voice.

"I bet Jack Frost has told you all about his plans," Kirsty went on. "He'd be sure to share them with a smart goblin like you."

"Oh yes, I know everything," said the goblin with a smug smile.

"Do tell us," said Kirsty. "After all, it doesn't matter now. You've kept us here past twelve o'clock."

"That's true," said the goblin cheerfully. "And from now on it's going to be *twice* as hard for you to get the better of Jack Frost!"

"What do you mean?" asked Myla.

"He stole the magical objects so that he could make his own twin," said the goblin, looking up at the fairies with a smirk. "Two Jack Frosts will be able to take over Fairyland forever!"

Myla gave a horrified gasp, and Lila let out a shocked cry.

"Can he do that?" asked Rachel.

"Our magical objects are very powerful," said Myla. "If he combines his magic with ours, he can use it to make a copy of himself."

"*Two* Jack Frosts?" said Kirsty. "One is bad enough – how can we stop two?"

"Let's go to the Ice Castle," said Lila, raising her wand. "Perhaps Jack Frost won't know how to use our magic. If we're lucky, we might still be in time to stop him!"

Twice the Ice

Lila and Myla put the tips of their wands together, and a double jet of pink fairy dust spiralled out. The glittering spiral wound around Rachel and Kirsty, lifting them into the air and shrinking them until they were the same size as the Twins Fairies. They felt glimmering wings grow on their backs, and then they were fluttering together against the roof of the shed.

"It's pointless," jeered the goblin, gazing up at them. "You can't stop him now."

"We'll see about that!" said Lila.

The fairies tapped their wands together twice, and Rachel and Kirsty were surrounded by a starburst of fairy dust. When the sparkles cleared, they were fluttering above the Ice Castle. Snow blanketed the ground, but for once the sun was shining and the girls were quite warm.

"I can see Jack Frost!" said Kirsty at once. "Look, he's in the main courtyard with all his goblins."

"Let's hide in one of the turrets and watch," said Rachel.

The girls had both been to the Ice Castle before, so they led the Twins Fairies to a turret from where they could see the courtyard. Jack Frost was standing in the middle of a gaggle of goblins.

"I can only see one Jack Frost," Myla whispered. "Perhaps his spell hasn't worked."

He was strutting up and down in front of something that was tall and thin, and covered in a red cloth.

"You are very lucky goblins," Jack Frost declared. "You are about to witness my greatest triumph!"

"Get your wand ready," Lila whispered to her twin. "When he casts his spell, we have to try to block it. If we work together, we should be strong enough to stop him."

But instead of raising his wand, he raised his hand and pulled on the red cover. Standing on a round platform was an exact copy of Jack Frost. The spell had already been done!

"My name is Jimmy Thaw," announced the twin. "I have come to rule over you, side by side with my brother Jack!"

The fairies gasped and several of the goblins squawked and screeched. One of them fainted, and there was a scrabble as several others tried to hide. Jack Frost cackled with pleasure.

"Behold the power of my magic!" he said, as Jimmy Thaw waved to the crowd of goblins and grinned at him. "But it is only right that I should thank those who have helped me, even if they are goody-two-shoes pesky fairies. I couldn't have done it without the help of Lila and Myla!"

"How could he say that?" cried Myla, her eyes filling with tears. "We haven't helped him!"

Lila put her arms around her twin and gave her a warm hug.

"We're going to stop him, and get our magical objects back," she said. "We've got Rachel and Kirsty to help us, so try not to worry."

Rachel and Kirsty exchanged a nervous smile. They hoped that they could match up to Lila's belief in them!

Just then, Jack Frost jabbed his finger at a nearby goblin, who was staring at the twin with his mouth hanging open.

"What are you waiting for?" Jack Frost bellowed. "Go and hide that fairy bauble *now*!"

The goblin gave a squeal of alarm and sprinted out of the castle.

"Look, he's got something in his hand!" said Rachel.

"It must be one of our magical objects," Myla exclaimed, brushing her tears away. "Come on, let's follow him!"

Magical Mimics

Led by Myla, the fairies zoomed out
of the turret and followed the goblin
as he ran away from the castle. They
flew high and saw him racing towards
the forest.

"We'll have to fly lower or else we'll
lose him among the trees," called Kirsty.

In single file, the fairies swooped down
and followed the goblin into the forest.

The sun had been making the snow-covered branches sparkle, but now that they were inside the forest, everything was dark and cold.

"I can hear the goblin up ahead," whispered Rachel. "Listen!"

There was a loud crashing and crunching up ahead, as if the goblin was blundering through thick bushes and losing his way. They flew as fast as they could, weaving through spiky branches and trying to keep up with him.

Suddenly, the crashing noises stopped.

"Oh no, I hope we haven't lost him," said Myla.

"No, don't worry," said Lila, who was in the lead. "He's stopped to catch his breath."

There was a little clearing up ahead, and the goblin was sitting on a boulder, huffing and puffing. The girls could see a delicate chain dangling from his hand, and something  dark pink was clutched in his fist.

"That's my half of the pendant!" Lila exclaimed. "Myla has the pale pink half, and mine is dark pink."

"How can we get it back?" asked Myla worriedly.

"Jack Frost's spell has given me an idea," said Rachel. "Perhaps if we all look like exact copies of the goblin, we can confuse him into giving back the pendant."

The Twins Fairies looked at each other and nodded.

"We think that's a brilliant idea," said Myla.

Rachel and Kirsty couldn't help but laugh at their reaction.

"Can you read each other's minds?" asked Kirsty.

"No," said Lila with a grin. "But we are so close that often we just know what the other is thinking!"

Myla and Lila linked their little fingers

and raised their wands at exactly the same time. Then they spoke the spell together:

"To stop Jack Frost
from causing trouble,
Make each of us
the goblin's double!"

There was a rush of icy wind that ruffled the girls' hair and made them shiver. Then their ears became pointy, their noses began to grow and their skin turned a sickly shade of green. Within a few seconds, they all looked exactly the same as the goblin in the clearing.

"Let me go first," said Rachel. "I'm going to annoy him by copying everything he does."

She crept closer to the goblin and waited until he was looking down. Then she stood in front of him. The goblin stood up and then jumped. Rachel jumped too.

"That's funny," he said to himself. "I don't remember seeing a mirror here before."

He preened himself and Rachel copied everything he did. Then Kirsty ran into the clearing and started to do a silly dance.

"Another mirror," gasped the goblin. "But this one's making me look stupid!

Stop it! I would never dance like that!"

Lila did a roly-
poly into the
clearing and
then jumped up
and pulled the
ugliest face she
could manage.

"EEK!" squealed
the goblin. "I don't do roly-polies and I
don't look like that! I'm tall, green and
handsome! Take these mirrors away, I
don't like them!"

He started to back away, and he
bumped into Myla.

"BOO!" she said when he turned
around in surprise.

"Help!" squealed the goblin, waving
his hands in the air.

All four copies started waving their hands in the air too, and shouting "Help! Help!" just like him. Finally the goblin flung the pendant down on the ground and kicked it away from him.

"I've had enough of that tricksy twin magic!" he howled. "I'm off!"

With a final squeal of alarm, he ran back into the forest. Lila and Myla swished their wands and turned them all back into fairies. Then Lila fluttered down, picked up her half of the pendant and fastened it around her neck.

"Hurray!" cheered Myla, hugging her twin. "Now Jack Frost can't make any more copies of himself."

Rachel and Kirsty clapped, and then they all held hands and danced into the air, twirling around in a glimmering fairy circle. It was great fun, but when they fluttered to the ground again, Lila looked serious.

"It's wonderful that we've got my pendant back, but we still need Myla's half and the Gemini ring to be able to help twins again," she said.

"Then we have to keep looking," said Rachel in a determined voice. "Don't worry, Myla. We'll find your pendant and stop Jack Frost's plans. I know we will!"

Myla's Pendant

Contents

An Icy Schoolroom

Rachel and Kirsty had helped the Twins Fairies to find one half of their missing pendant, but the other half and the Gemini ring were still missing.

"We have to stop Jack Frost from causing any more mischief," said Kirsty.

"He'll be planning all sorts of trouble now he has his own twin," Rachel added solemnly.

With a determined nod, Lila zoomed up through the dense trees.

"Come on!" she called over her shoulder. "If we go back to the Ice Castle, we might find a clue to where he's hidden our other magical objects!"

The castle turrets were topped with snow and a grey snow cloud was hovering overhead. But when the friends reached the courtyard, the huge crowd of goblins had disappeared. There were just a few goblin guards leaning against the courtyard wall and squabbling. The

fairies fluttered together and Rachel
pointed to an opening on one side of the
courtyard. A guard was standing beside
it, yawning.

"That's the way to the Throne Room,"
Rachel whispered. "I remember from
when we were here before."

"But how are we going to get past the
guard?" asked Kirsty.

"I've got a little idea," said Lila with a twinkle in her eyes. "He looks a bit sleepy, don't you think?"

Myla giggled and raised her wand.

"Sometimes it's as if Lila and I can read each other's mind," she told the girls.

She waved her wand and cast a silent spell. A little stream of shimmering fairy dust coiled out of her wand and wound around the goblin guard's head. He gave another enormous yawn and then slid down the wall, fast asleep.

Rachel and Kirsty had to put their hands over their mouths to stifle their giggles!

"Lead the way to the Throne Room," Lila whispered to them. "We have to find Jack Frost."

Rachel and Kirsty zoomed into the dark entrance, followed by Lila and Myla. They fluttered through a maze of damp, smelly corridors, hearing only the steady drip of water.

At last they reached the door of the
Throne Room. It was
slightly ajar, and
someone inside
was shouting
loudly.

"That's Jack
Frost," Kirsty
whispered.

"Call yourself
an Ice Lord?" he was
bellowing. "You'll be in detention for a
month if you don't get this right! Now
I'll give you one more chance. What do
you do when you see a fairy?"

"Ask them if they'd like a cup of tea?"
replied a friendly voice.

"If you see a fairy, you steal her
magical objects!" Jack Frost roared.

"Repeat this after me…

"When you and I rule Fairyland,
All pesky fairies will be banned!"

Myla beckoned the
others and slipped
through the
opening into
the Throne
Room. Lila
was close
behind her,
followed by
Rachel and Kirsty.
There was a wooden chair beside the
door, and each of them hid behind one
of its legs. Then they gazed around in
amazement.

71

   The Throne Room had been
decorated to look like a school
classroom. There was a large table in
front of the throne, and Jack Frost was
wearing an old-fashioned teacher's cap
and gown. Facing the throne, Jimmy
Thaw was sitting at a small desk. The
goblins were sitting in neat rows on the
floor behind him.

"But what's so bad about fairies?" asked Jimmy Thaw.

Jack Frost thumped the desk in front of him, and his cap slipped to one side.

"We're not leaving this room until you agree to help me take over Fairyland!" he shouted.

Fairies in Hiding

The goblins started to wail.

"I'm hungry!" squawked one.

"The floor's too hard!" another cried.

Jimmy Thaw turned to look at them.

"Poor things," he said. "Let's stop for a spot of tea and find some cushions for them to sit on."

The goblins were gazing at him with adoring eyes, but Jack Frost turned purple with fury.

"No tea!" he shouted. "No cushions!"

Lila turned to the others, her eyes sparkling with fun.

"It looks as if Jack Frost isn't enjoying having a twin as much as he expected!" she whispered.

Jack Frost took a deep breath.

"Listen," he said, "You're not here to talk about cushions."

"Of course not," said Jimmy Thaw in a polite voice. "I'm glad to hear you say that, because there are a few other things I'd like to talk about."

"Yes," said Jack Frost, rubbing his bony hands together and sniggering. "There's lots of plotting and planning to be done."

"I'm good at planning," said Jimmy Thaw. "First, I think the whole castle could do with a coat of paint. We should turn on the central heating too – it's a bit chilly."

Jack Frost's mouth dropped open, but his twin didn't seem to notice.

"Oh, and I'd like to talk about fair wages for the goblins," Jimmy Frost went on.

The goblins were shuffling closer and closer to Jimmy Thaw. One very small goblin was sitting on his foot.

"I love you," whispered the little goblin.

Jimmy Thaw patted him on the head
and Jack Frost glowered, pulling at
something around his neck.

"*I'm* his twin," the fairies heard
Jack Frost mutter. "He should like *me*
best of all."

"I think he's jealous," said Rachel.

"Look!" whispered Kirsty. "He's
taking something from
around his neck."

Myla gave an
excited gasp.

"It's my half
of the pendant!"
she said.

Jack Frost held
up the pendant
and then put it around
Jimmy Thaw's neck.

79

"This is a present for you," he said.
"But you must never take it off, and
always keep it safe from the fairies."

"Thank you very
much!" said
Jimmy Thaw.

Kirsty turned
to the others.

"This is our
chance," she
whispered.
"Jimmy
Thaw seems
really nice. If we
explain to him that
the pendant is stolen, perhaps he will
return it."

Rachel, Lila and Myla nodded, but
then Jack Frost spoke again.

"We'll continue your meanness lessons later," he said with a scowl. "Goblins, look after my twin and give him whatever he wants, OR ELSE!"

"He's coming this way!" Myla squeaked excitedly.

As Jack Frost strode past the fairies' hiding place, his flowing cloak caught Rachel's wings and knocked her down. She tumbled out from under the chair – right into the middle of the room!

Luckily, no one had seen her. The goblins were all gazing at Jimmy Thaw, and he was looking at the pendant around his neck. Rachel was safe. She zoomed into the air, and the others flew up to join her.

"How are we going to talk to Jimmy Thaw in private?" asked Myla. "Those goblins don't want to leave his side!"

Distracted Goblins

Just then, Jimmy Thaw stood up and yawned.

"I'm tired," he said. "I think I'll go to my room for a little snooze."

The fairies looked around at each other in excitement.

"Perhaps this could be our chance," Lila whispered.

But the goblins had stood up too.

"We'll come with you," said the smallest goblin.

The procession set off though the castle. There were two goblins walking ahead of Jimmy Thaw, two beside him and two behind him. The fairies fluttered along above their heads, trying to think of a way to speak to Jimmy Thaw alone.

After they had followed the procession along three corridors and up two flights of stairs, Lila groaned.

"This is impossible!" she said.
"The goblins are never going to leave
him alone."

"Maybe we can *tempt* them away
from him somehow," said Rachel.

"Good thinking, Rachel," said Myla.
"I've got an idea!"

She waved her
wand, and two
green yo-yos
rolled out of
the shadows
towards the
last goblins
in the
procession.
They stopped and picked them up.

"I'm brilliant at yo-yoing," said one.

"Not as good as me!" said the other.

Glaring at each other, the goblins started a yo-yo competition. They forgot all about following the others.

"That was great, Myla," said Kirsty with a giggle.

"Watch this!" said Lila.

She waved her wand, and two delicious-smelling pasties appeared on a plate at the side of the corridor. Lila sent the smell drifting towards the two goblins next to Jimmy Thaw in the procession.

They stopped and sniffed the air.

"What's that?" whispered one.

"Look!" said the other, pointing at the pasties. "Yummy!"

They scurried over to the pasties and started to gobble them up.

"Four down, two to go," said Rachel. "What shall we try next?"

"Lila, could you make me sound like Jack Frost?" Kirsty suggested. "I've got an idea."

Lila gave a wink and waved her wand.

"Has it worked?" she asked.

"How do I sound?" whispered Kirsty.

The others giggled.

"You sound exactly like Jack Frost!" said Lila.

"Except that we're not used to hearing Jack Frost whisper," Rachel added.

Kirsty grinned and fluttered down until she was flying along beside the ear of one of the goblins. It was so dark in the corridor that he didn't see her.

"You, goblin!" she said in Jack Frost's voice. "Get back to the Throne Room and polish my desk!"

The goblin jumped and scurried back towards the Throne Room. Kirsty flew back to the others, smiling, and Lila returned her voice to normal. Jimmy

Thaw and his goblin companion
walked straight ahead to the door of
a turret bedroom.

"This is my room," said Jimmy Thaw.
"Time for a little nap."

The fairies followed Jimmy Thaw
and the goblin into the turret bedroom.
Jimmy Thaw sat on the end of the bed
and the Twins Fairies groaned. The
goblin wasn't going to leave Jimmy
Thaw alone!

A Sleepy Song

"Can you girls try to distract the goblin so we can talk to Jimmy Thaw?" asked Lila.

"We'll do our best!" whispered Rachel.

While Jimmy Thaw stretched and plumped up his pillows, the goblin gave a yawn and sank into an uncomfortable-looking chair beside the window. Rachel and Kirsty hid in a fold of the curtain beside him.

"He's not taking his eyes off Jimmy Thaw," said Rachel.

"Do you remember the sleeping spell that Myla cast earlier?" Kirsty whispered. "Perhaps we could try that."

"But we can't do magic," said Rachel.

"No," agreed Kirsty, "but perhaps he might drop off to sleep if we sing him a lullaby!"

From behind the curtain, the girls began to sing in soft voices. The goblin's eyelids drooped, flickered and drooped again. Rachel and Kirsty kept singing, and at last the goblin's eyes closed.

"He's asleep!" said Rachel.

Together with the Twins Fairies, they fluttered out in front of Jimmy Thaw, who was just settling back onto his pillows.

"Good heavens!" he exclaimed. "Are you fairies?"

"Yes," said Lila. "We're the Twins Fairies, and these are our friends Rachel and Kirsty. We've come to ask you to return something that belongs to us."

Quickly, the fairies told Jimmy Thaw
how Jack Frost had stolen their magical
objects. Jimmy Thaw's eyes opened
very wide and he touched the pendant
around his neck.

"You're saying that this necklace is
stolen?" he asked.

"Yes," said Rachel. "It belongs to
Myla. Lila has the other half – look."

Lila showed him her half of the
pendant.

"Well, if this belongs to you then of course you can have it back," he said at once. "But I think there must be some sort of misunderstanding. I can't believe my twin is really that naughty."

"He is very naughty indeed, and so are all his goblins," said Kirsty.

"There's only one thing we can do," said Jimmy Thaw, standing up. "We're going to find Jack and ask him for an explanation!"

"Please, don't go to Jack Frost!" cried Rachel. "He mustn't know we're here!"

"He'll try to capture us!" said Myla.

"No, no," said Jimmy Thaw, waving his hand. "He's just joking when he says things like that. Don't worry, we'll soon get this cleared up and then we'll all have a nice cup of tea."

He marched out of the room and the fairies darted after him. They sped through the corridors and down the stairs, pleading with him to stop. But when he reached the door of the Throne Room he pushed it open and strode inside.

Jack Frost was sitting on his throne, but he jumped to his feet when he saw his twin and the fairies.

"What's going on?" he bellowed.

"There seems to have been a little mix-up," said Jimmy Thaw. "These fairies say that the pendant you gave me belongs to them. I'm sure you can explain everything."

Jack Frost clenched his fists.

"Of course I can explain!" he yelled. "I took it, so it's MINE!"

99

Jimmy Thaw stared at him in shock. "But stealing is wrong," he said.

He took the pendant from around his neck and held it out to Myla. Jack Frost let out a howl of anger as Myla took it and placed it around her neck.

"You might have got it, but you won't keep it!" said Jack Frost, glaring at the fairies. "Goblins, don't let any of them out of this room!"

Jimmy Thaw Takes Sides

Some of the goblins raced across the room to block the doorway, while others leapt into the air to try to catch the fairies. Rachel, Kirsty, Lila and Myla fluttered out of their reach.

"Try the windows!" called Lila.

They zoomed around the room, but all the windows were closed. Fluttering above the goblins' grasping hands, they looked at each other in alarm.

"We can't get out," said Rachel. "What shall we do?"

Jack Frost looked up at them and a cruel smile spread across his face.

"I'll make you a deal," he said. "I'll let you go if you give me the pendant."

"Never!" squeaked Myla.

"No way!" added her twin, folding her arms across her chest.

"Then you'll never leave my Throne Room!" Jack Frost yelled. "Goblins, get that pendant!"

The goblins started to stand on each other's shoulders, creating living ladders that swayed across the room. The fairies were forced to press themselves against the ceiling, but the goblins just kept climbing and making more ladders.

The room was filling up with them.

"There's no escape!" cried Kirsty.

"Goblins," said a
gentle voice. "Dear
goblins, please
listen to me."

It was Jimmy
Thaw. The
goblins turned
to look at him.
Two of them lost
their balance, and
they all fell over.

"You are all tired and hungry," he
said. "Why waste your energy trying to
catch these poor little fairies? Let's all go
to the kitchen and have a feast!"

The goblins cheered and Jack Frost
stamped his foot.

"If you let those fairies go, I'll punish you all for a YEAR!" he shouted.

"Forget about the fairies, and ignore my grumpy twin," Jimmy Thaw told the goblins. "This is my home too, and I say it's feast time. Come on, goblins – let the fairies go!"

With whoops and cheers, the goblins darted around the room, flinging open the windows.

"Go!" cried Jimmy Thaw to the fairies. "Good luck!"

"Thank you!" called the fairies.

One by one, they swooped out through a window. In a few seconds, Rachel, Kirsty, Lila and Myla were hovering high above the Ice Castle.  The angry yells of Jack Frost and the excited squeals of the goblins were ringing in their ears.

"We did it!" cheered Lila, spinning around in delight. "Now we have both halves of the pendant. Hurray!"

"That means everything should be back to normal at your friend's party," said Myla to the girls. "We'll send you back so that you can enjoy the fun."

"But what about the Gemini ring?" asked Rachel. "Jack Frost still has that."

"We'll come and find you soon to help us look for it," Lila promised. "But now it's party time for you!"

She waved her wand, and there was a dazzling flash of sparkling light. When the sparkles cleared, Rachel and Kirsty were back in Jessy and Amy's garden. They could hear happy shouts and laughter coming from the house.

"Of course, no time has passed since we left," said Kirsty. "That's one of the most exciting things about visiting Fairyland!"

"Come on," said Rachel. "Let's go and see if finding Myla's pendant has made a difference."

They ran up to the house and hurried back through the kitchen into the sitting room. Everyone was playing Pass the Parcel, and Jessy smiled at them.

"Come and join the game," she said. "Mum and Dad found the missing prizes – someone had moved them by mistake."

"And there are still going to be two parties," added her mum with a smile. "I don't know what made us consider cancelling one!"

Rachel and Kirsty shared a secret glance as they sat down. They knew exactly what had gone wrong!

"I hope we can find the Gemini ring soon," Kirsty whispered. "Without the Twins Fairies, there could still be trouble at Amy's party."

The music began and the parcel started to make its way around the circle. Rachel squeezed Kirsty's hand.

"I'm sure we'll be able to help," she said. "But right now we've got a party game to play!"

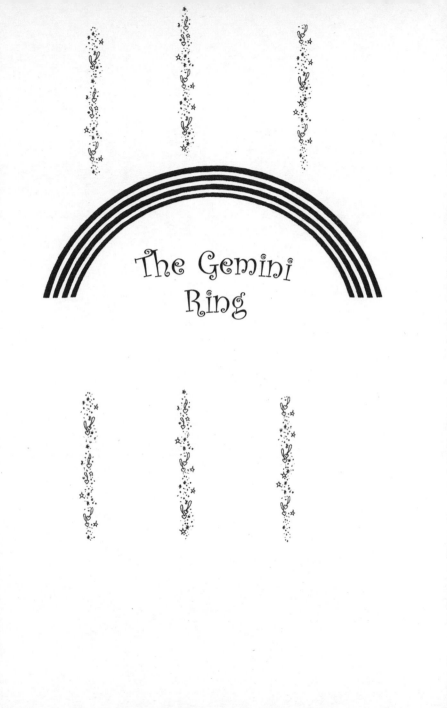

The Gemini
Ring

Contents

Brand-new Twins

"Higher!" shouted Kirsty, in between giggles.

Rachel pushed her tree swing again and Kirsty flew into the air.

"Your feet touched the branches then!" said Rachel, laughing.

"Higher!" Kirsty urged.

Rachel pushed as hard as she could, and Kirsty flew into the air again. This time, she seemed to stay up for ages. When she came down there was a flurry of golden sparkles, and the Twins Fairies were sitting on her lap!

"We've got some news!" said Myla in an excited voice.

She flew off Kirsty's lap and perched on Rachel's shoulder.

"There's a big twins research conference starting today," said Lila.

"They're holding a garden party, and there will be lots of twins there."

"Oh dear," said Kirsty. "Without the Gemini ring, that could be a disaster."

"Exactly," said Myla. "But this afternoon, Jimmy Thaw came to the Fairyland Palace."

"What did he want?" asked Rachel.

"He came to tell us that Jack Frost is

going to the conference to try to find
out how to make the two of them more
alike," said Lila. "But Jimmy Thaw
doesn't want to be like him, so he has
promised to meet us there and help us to
get the ring back!"

"That's wonderful!" Kirsty exclaimed,
jumping down from the swing. "Let's
go!"

"We hoped
you'd say
that," said
Myla, fluttering
into the air.
"Ready, Lila?"

In perfect unison,
the Twins Fairies
raised their wands and
waved them in a figure of

eight. There was a burst of glimmering fairy dust, and then Rachel and Kirsty heard a whooshing sound. They blinked, and found themselves standing at the entrance gate of a large garden, beside a big sign.

TWINS CONFERENCE GARDEN PARTY
Research scientists and twins only!

"Oh no," said Myla. "How can Kirsty and Rachel get inside?"

"You could turn us into fairies," Kirsty suggested.

"I've got a better idea," said Lila. "How about you and Rachel become twins?"

Rachel and Kirsty exchanged a thrilled glance.

"Yes, please!" they said together.

Lila laughed.

"You're already starting to sound like twins!" she said, raising her wand. "Come on, Myla."

Together, the Twins Fairies spoke the words of a very special spell:

Peas in pods and mirrors bright,
Match these girls in weight and height.
Copy every lock of hair,
And make them seem a perfect pair.

The girls were transformed in the twinkling of an eye. They stared at each other in amazement.

"We've both got your ponytail," said Kirsty with a giggle.

"But our hair is dark like yours," said Rachel, smiling.

Rachel was wearing a stripy top and Kirsty had a matching stripy skirt. Their shoes were exactly the same, and over their shoulders were matching bags.

They squeezed each other's hand and shared a smile. Just then, one of the conference organisers hurried past them.

"Come along, twins!" he said. "You'll be late for the party!"

Twin Tempers

Lila hid inside Rachel's bag and Myla slipped into Kirsty's bag. Then the girls hurried into the private garden. There were rows of neatly clipped hedges and several beautifully arranged flowerbeds.

"I can hear voices," said Kirsty.

There was a loud buzz of chatter coming from the centre of the garden. Rachel and Kirsty hurried towards the sound. In the middle of the garden was a pretty little square surrounded by bay trees. There was a small crowd of people chatting and sipping drinks. Waiters and

waitresses were walking around with
trays of snacks.

"Look at all the twins!" said Rachel
with a gasp.

Each pair of twins was dressed in the
same clothes. It was amazing to see
double of everyone!

"Those must be the scientists," said
Kirsty, looking at a few people
dressed in suits. "None of them seems
to have a twin."

"Let's join the party," said Rachel.

They walked up to a group of twins
who were chatting to a scientist.

"So you don't like being twins?" said
the scientist, looking surprised.

"Everyone compares us to each other," moaned one boy.

"People don't treat us as individuals," a girl complained.

"And we always have to share everything," grumbled her twin. "It's really annoying."

Lila popped her head out of Rachel's shoulder bag.

"These twins should be happy to be part of the conference," she whispered. "They are feeling unhappy because our Gemini ring is still missing. We have to find it or the conference will be ruined!"

The girls walked on and heard another of the scientists talking to a couple of lady twins.

"The truth is that you are cleverer and prettier than your twin," he said to one of them.

Myla peeped out of Kirsty's bag and gave a shocked gasp.

"No one should ever say that to

twins!" she exclaimed. "A scientist should know better. It must be because of the ring being missing. Oh dear, what are we going to do?"

"Without the ring, twins will be compared with each other all the time," said Lila. "That will make them miserable."

Rachel and Kirsty could tell how anxious both the Twins Fairies were feeling.

"Please don't worry," said Kirsty. "Remember, Jimmy Thaw has promised to help us. We will get the ring back and stop Jack Frost's naughty plans."

Just then, Rachel let out a squeak of excitement.

"I can see Jack Frost!" she said. "He's over there by the statue, talking to one of the scientists."

Beside a white statue of a dolphin, Jack Frost was standing very close to a short, plump scientist. She was standing with her back against a hedge, but she couldn't get any further away from him. It was obvious that she wanted to escape. Jimmy Thaw was standing a few steps away, looking very embarrassed.

"Let's get closer," said Kirsty. "We might be able to hear what he's saying."

They edged closer, trying to stay out of Jack Frost's view. But he only had eyes for the scientist.

"Listen to me," he was saying in a loud voice. "I'm sick of my twin being different from me. I want us to be exactly the same, and you are going to tell me how. Now!"

"But – but – but…" the scientist stammered.

Kirsty caught Jimmy Thaw's eye and he gave her a little smile. Then he pointed to his little finger and to Jack Frost.

"What does he mean?" Rachel whispered to Lila.

"I know!" said the fairy in an excited voice. "He means that Jack Frost has the Gemini ring on his little finger. It's here!"

An Icy Prison

"I really must go and speak to someone about…er…something…" said the scientist.

She ducked under Jack Frost's arm and hurried off into the crowd. Jack Frost turned, and the girls darted behind a hedge. They saw him turn on Jimmy Thaw and poke him in the chest with one long, bony finger.

"I'm going to find a scientist who can turn you into me, if it takes me all day!" he shouted. "There's something wrong with you, the way you keep going on about being nice to fairies!"

Jimmy Thaw hung his head and looked miserable.

"Why does Jack Frost have to be so mean?" asked Myla.

Her eyes brimmed with tears of pity for Jimmy Thaw, and Lila suddenly shot into the air.

"I won't let him upset anyone any

more," she said in a fierce voice. "Wait here – I'm going to get our ring back!"

Before anyone could stop her, Lila was zooming towards Jack Frost. She hovered behind the statue so that no one else at the party could see her. Then she folded her arms and glared at him.

"Give us back our ring," she said. "It doesn't belong to you."

Jack Frost narrowed his eyes into bad-tempered slits.

"I don't take orders from fairies!" he snarled nastily.

He raised his wand and hurled an ice bolt at Lila. She dodged it, but he blasted another one and it hit her with a blue flash. Her wand flew into the air and Jack Frost caught it.

"No!" cried Myla.

Lila was trapped inside a tiny cage of

ice, no bigger than an egg. She shook the freezing bars, but they were too strong for her little hands.

"Let me go!" she exclaimed.

The ice cage dropped into Jack Frost's hand, and he slipped it and Lila's wand into his pocket.

"That'll teach those pesky fairies a lesson!" he told Jimmy Thaw.

Rachel and Kirsty could hardly believe what they had just seen. Myla was terribly upset. She started to shiver.

"We have to rescue Lila," she cried. "She's cold in that ice cage – I can feel it too."

"How can we get her back without Jack Frost seeing us?" asked Rachel.

"We can't," said Kirsty. "We have to be cleverer than that. I've got an idea. Myla, can you make me look like one of the scientists?"

Myla looked surprised, but she nodded and waved her wand. Kirsty's stripy outfit was replaced by a dark blue suit, and her hair was scraped back into a tight bun. Thick-framed glasses disguised her face.

"What's your plan?" asked Rachel.

"No time to explain," said Kirsty. "I have to try to set Lila free."

She hurried over to Jack Frost and tapped him on the shoulder. He turned and scowled at her.

"I couldn't help overhearing you earlier," she said, trying not to sound too nervous. "I think I can help."

Jack Frost grabbed her shoulder in a tight grip.

"You can make my twin exactly the same as me?"

"I can make everything as it should be," said Kirsty. "I just need to use my special scanner."

She put her hand into her pocket and glanced over to Myla's hiding place.

She needed something that looked like a scanner – quickly!

Tricked!

Myla understood immediately. She waved her wand and a small, square piece of metal appeared in Kirsty's hand. It was bleeping and flashing with green lights. It looked very important. Kirsty held it out in front of her and ran it up and down Jack Frost's body. Then she did the same to Jimmy Thaw.

"Aha, I see," she said.

"What is it?" demanded Jack Frost. "Tell me!"

"My scanner tells me that something is stopping you from connecting as twins should," she said. "There is something very powerful about the ring you are wearing on your finger."

Jack Frost narrowed his eyes and put his hand behind his back to hide the magical Gemini ring.

"You're not having it," he snapped.

"Goodness me, of course not!" said Kirsty, sounding as shocked as she could. "It doesn't belong to me, so that would be stealing. No, all you need to do is put the ring on your twin's finger. Then he will share its power."

Jack Frost's eyes lit up with excitement, and he started to tug at the ring.

"Oh, there's just one other thing," said Kirsty in a casual voice. "When you hand over the ring, make sure that you are not carrying anything very cold, like a lolly or an ice cube. That could stop the ring from working properly."

Jack Frost thrust his hand into his pocket, pulled out the ice cage and shoved it into Kirsty's hand, along with the tiny wand.

"Hold that," he said.

Kirsty held it, not daring to release Lila until the ring was safe. Jack Frost pulled the ring off his finger and gave it to Jimmy Thaw.

"Put it on!" he ordered.

Jimmy Thaw looked around and Kirsty drew in her breath. Of course, he didn't recognise her! The last time he saw her she had been a fairy, and now she was

in disguise. Jimmy Thaw started to put
the ring on his finger and Kirsty bit her
lip. As soon as Jack Frost realised that it
wasn't working, he would want the ring
back. Her plan was going wrong!

"Wait!" cried a tiny voice.

Myla darted out of
her hiding place
and zoomed
above Jimmy
Thaw's head.
He looked up
with a smile,
and Jack Frost
flapped his hands
at her.

"Shoo, fairy pest!"
he said. "You're too late!"

"Oh no she isn't," said his twin.

He held the ring
high above his
head, and Myla
swooped down
and took it.
Immediately it
shrank to fairy size,
and Myla slipped it
onto her finger.

"NO!" shrieked
Jack Frost.

Just then, Lila fluttered into the air,
taking out her wand and shaking drops
of water from her wings. The warmth
of Kirsty's hand had melted her prison
away. Jack Frost's eyes looked as if they
might pop out of his head. He jumped
up and down on the spot, his fists
clenched. Rachel came out of her hiding

place and Jack Frost's eyes widened.

"What's going on?" he asked in a choked voice.

Myla waved her wand and Kirsty and Rachel were transformed back into their normal selves.

"YOU!" spluttered Jack Frost.

"Yes, it's us," said Rachel. "You should know by now that whenever you cause trouble for the fairies, we won't be far away."

"You told me that my twin would share the ring's power if I gave it to him," Jack Frost said to Kirsty angrily. "You lied!"

"No, I told the truth," said Kirsty in a firm voice. "Jimmy Thaw *did* share the ring's power – with its rightful owners!"

Goodbyes

Myla and Lila hugged each other and Rachel and Kirsty jumped up and down in excitement. Now that the Twins Fairies had their magical objects back, everything would go back to normal for twins around the world.

"There's just one thing left to do," said Lila, looking sadly at Jimmy Thaw. "We have to send you back to where you came from."

"What does that mean?" asked Rachel. "Where do you come from?"

"Why," said Jimmy Thaw, "I come from Jack Frost."

"But that means you won't exist any more," said Kirsty. "Couldn't you stay?"

Jimmy Thaw shook his head kindly.

"I don't belong here," he said. "But it's all right. I am part of Jack Frost – do you understand what that means?"

The girls shook their heads.

"It means that Jack Frost isn't all bad," said Myla with a smile. "Jimmy Thaw is somewhere inside his heart!"

Together, the Twins Fairies waved their wands. Jimmy Thaw became a turquoise, twinkling blur of light, which coiled through the air and disappeared into Jack Frost's chest.

"It's not fair!" wailed Jack Frost, stamping his foot.

There was a bright flash of lightning and he disappeared, still scowling.

The girls hugged each
other and smiled at
the fairies, who
fluttered to their
shoulders.

"Listen," said
Myla in a low
voice.

The chatter
from the conference
guests suddenly
sounded brighter. The twins were smiling
and laughing, and Rachel and Kirsty
could hear odd snatches of conversation.

"Being a twin is a lot of fun!" one
woman was saying.

"There's always someone to play
with," said a little boy, putting his arm
around his twin's shoulders.

"Yes, we swap clothes all the time," said a teenage girl.

"And we play practical jokes on our friends," added a man with a grin.

"We did it!" cheered Lila, spinning giddily into the air.

"Come down," said Myla, giggling at her twin's excitement. "You'll be seen! Besides, we have to take Rachel and Kirsty home."

Lila came down laughing, and in a flurry of golden twinkles they were all transported back to Rachel's garden.

They heard Mrs Walker's voice calling from the back door of the house.

"Rachel! Kirsty! It's time to get ready for the party!"

The Twins Fairies each gave Rachel and Kirsty a delicate butterfly kiss.

"Without you we couldn't have found our magical objects," said Myla. "Thank you so much."

"Goodbye, and thank you," said Lila. "Remember us, and have fun at the party!"

Waving happily, the Twins Fairies vanished, leaving a little cloud of fairy dust hanging in the air.

"Look!" exclaimed Rachel, pointing at the wooden swing.

Two pink velvet boxes were lying on the seat. One was marked "Kirsty" and the other "Rachel" in golden letters.

"They must be presents from Lila and Myla," said Kirsty.

The girls opened the boxes and saw two halves of a long silver pendant, exactly like the one that the Twins Fairies shared.

"How beautiful," Rachel exclaimed. "We can wear them at the party."

They fastened the pendants around their necks and smiled at each other.

"Rachel, do you ever wish you had a twin?" Kirsty asked.

Rachel smiled and shook her head.

"I've got someone just as wonderful as a twin," she said. "I've got the best friend in the world!"

The End

Now it's time for Kirsty and
Rachel to help...

Kayla the Pottery Fairy

Read on for a sneak peek...

"I can see Rainspell Island!" Rachel
cried as the ferry sailed across the blue-
green sea, foamy waves slapping against
its sides. Ahead of them was a rocky
island with soaring cliffs and crescents of
golden sandy beaches around the coast.
"Not far now, Kirsty."

"Aren't we lucky, Rachel?" Kirsty said,
her face alight with excitement. "We
came here not long ago for the music
festival, and now we're back again for
Crafts Week!"

"And maybe some fairy adventures,
too?" Rachel murmured hopefully.

"Maybe, if we're *very* lucky," said Kirsty.

The girls had met for the first time when their families had both holidayed on Rainspell Island, and whilst exploring the island together, they'd made an amazing discovery. They'd found a tiny fairy called Ruby, and ever since then, Rachel and Kirsty had been loyal friends of the fairies. The girls had offered to help their magical friends many times when selfish Jack Frost and his naughty goblins were causing chaos in Fairyland.

The ferry docked at the jetty, and the girls' parents came up from below deck with all the luggage.

"That's our taxi," Mr Tate said, pointing out a people carrier waiting on the jetty.

"Mum said you can come and stay with us at the B and B for a few nights, Rachel," Kirsty remarked as they left the ferry.

"And you can come and stay at the campsite with us," Rachel added eagerly. "It'll be fun!"

Once the luggage had been packed into the taxi, the driver set off for Mimosa Cottage, the bed and breakfast where the Tates were staying. Rainspell Island was looking especially green and gorgeous, Rachel thought. It was spring and the wildflowers were in full bloom.

Very soon they arrived at Mimosa Cottage, a pretty little house with a thatched roof.

"Mum, can I go to the campsite with Rachel?" Kirsty asked as the taxi driver unloaded their suitcases.

"Of course," Mrs Tate replied. "We'll come and collect you later."

The campsite was a little further down the road in a large field. Rachel and Kirsty jumped out of the taxi, thrilled to see that Mr and Mrs Walker had hired one of the biggest tents on the site.

Read **Kayla the Pottery Fairy** to find out what adventures are in store for Kirsty and Rachel!

Meet the fairies, play games
and get sneak peeks at
the latest books!

There's fairy fun for everyone at

www.rainbowmagicbooks.co.uk

You'll find great activities, competitions, stories and
fairy profiles, and also a special newsletter.

Win Rainbow Magic Goodies!

There are lots of Rainbow Magic fairies, and we want to know which one is your favourite! Send us a picture of her and tell us in thirty words why she is your favourite and why you like Rainbow Magic books. Each month we will put the entries into a draw and select one winner to receive a Rainbow Magic Sparkly T-shirt and Goody Bag!

Send your entry on a postcard to Rainbow Magic Competition, Orchard Books, 338 Euston Road, London NW1 3BH.
Australian readers should email: childrens.books@hachette.com.au
New Zealand readers should write to Rainbow Magic Competition, PO Box 3255, Shortland St, Auckland 1140, NZ.
Don't forget to include your name and address.
Only one entry per child.

Good luck!

Tilly the Teacher Fairy

Meet Tilly the Teacher Fairy! Can Rachel and Kirsty help get her magical items back from Jack Frost and make school fun for everyone again?

www.rainbowmagicbooks.co.uk